DELTA FORCE

ASHLEY GISH

SPECIAL FORCES BOOKS

CREATIVE EDUCATION · CREATIVE PAPERBACKS

Published by Creative Education and Creative Paperbacks · P.O. Box 227, Mankato, Minnesota 56002 · Creative Education and Creative Paperbacks are imprints of The Creative Company · www.thecreativecompany.us · Design by Rita Marshall · Production by Dana Koehler · Printed in the USA · Photographs by 123RF (zabelin), Alamy (AA Film Archive/SCOTT FREE PRODUCTIONS/Sportsphoto, Michael Dwyer, Serge Mouraret, United Archives GmbH, US Navy Photo, A. T. Willett), Alchetron, Creative Commons Wikimedia (PO[Phot] Sean Clee/MOD, Ted Psahos/U.S. Immigration and Customs Enforcement/United States Department of Homeland Security, U.S. Army photo by Spc. Nikayla Shodeen/DVIDS), FreeVectorMaps.com, iStockphoto (FrozenShutter, Vesnaandjic, zabelin), Shutterstock (Bumble Dee, Getmilitaryphotos, Stephen Marques, New Africa, PRESSLAB)

Library of Congress Cataloging-in-Publication Data • Names: Gish, Ashley, author. • Title: Delta Force / Ashley Gish. • Series: X-Books: Special Forces. • Includes bibliographical references and index. • Summary: A countdown of five of the most fascinating Delta Force achievements provides thrills as readers learn about the training, skills, and gear utilized by this elite special operations force. • Identifiers: LCCN 2019051886 / ISBN 978-1-64026-369-7 (hardcover) / ISBN 978-1-62832-901-8 (pbk) / ISBN 978-1-64000-523-5 (eBook) • LCSH: United States. Army. Delta Force—History—Juvenile literature. / Special forces (Military science)—United States—Juvenile literature.

Classification: LCC UA34.S64 G568 2021 / DDC 356/.1670973—dc23

CCSS: RI.3.1-8; RI.4.1-5, 7; RI.5.1-3, 8; RI.6.1-2, 4, 7; RH.6-8.3-8

First Edition HC 9 8 7 6 5 4 3 2 1 • First Edition PBK 9 8 7 6 5 4 3 2 1

DELTA FORCE

CONTENTS

DELTA FORCE RECRUITS

UNITED STATES ARMY
UNITED STATES MARINE CORPS
UNITED STATES NAVY
UNITED STATES AIR FORCE
UNITED STATES COAST GUARD

XTRAORDINARY FORCE

Delta Force is an elite unit of the United States armed forces. It carries out secret operations all over the globe. Delta Force recruits troops from all branches of the military.

Delta Force Basics

Delta Force is highly specialized. Its operators primarily focus on counterterrorism. They capture terrorists and prevent them from carrying out attacks. Delta Force also protects military officers and foreign leaders. The unit rescues hostages, too.

Most Delta Force operators come from other special forces units. They receive little to no recognition for their work. But they do not mind. Secrecy is celebrated among Delta Force operators. They are proud to work in the shadows to keep people safe.

DELTA FORCE

Delta Force headquarters are located at Fort Bragg, North Carolina. The unit participates in secret missions around the globe.

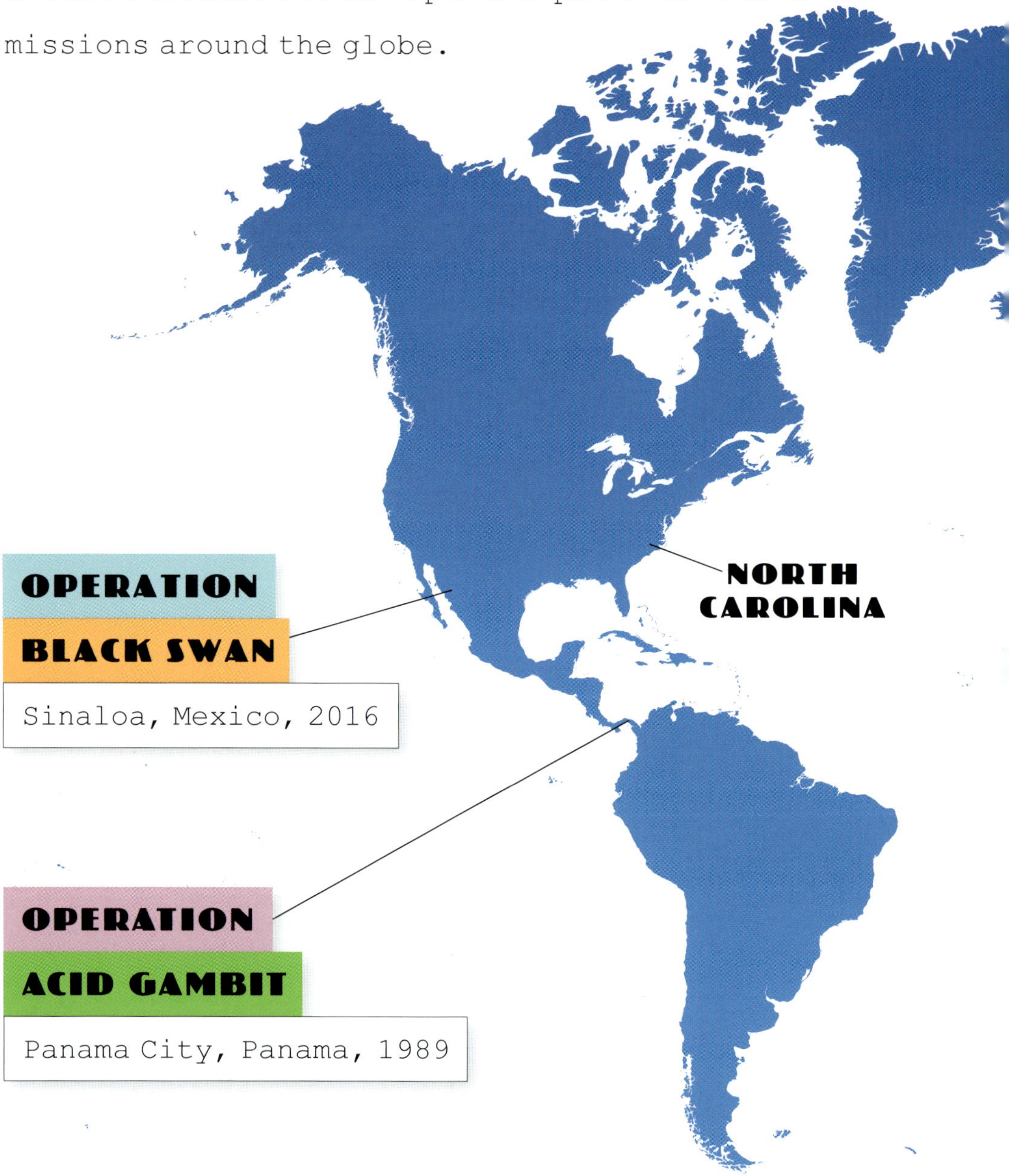

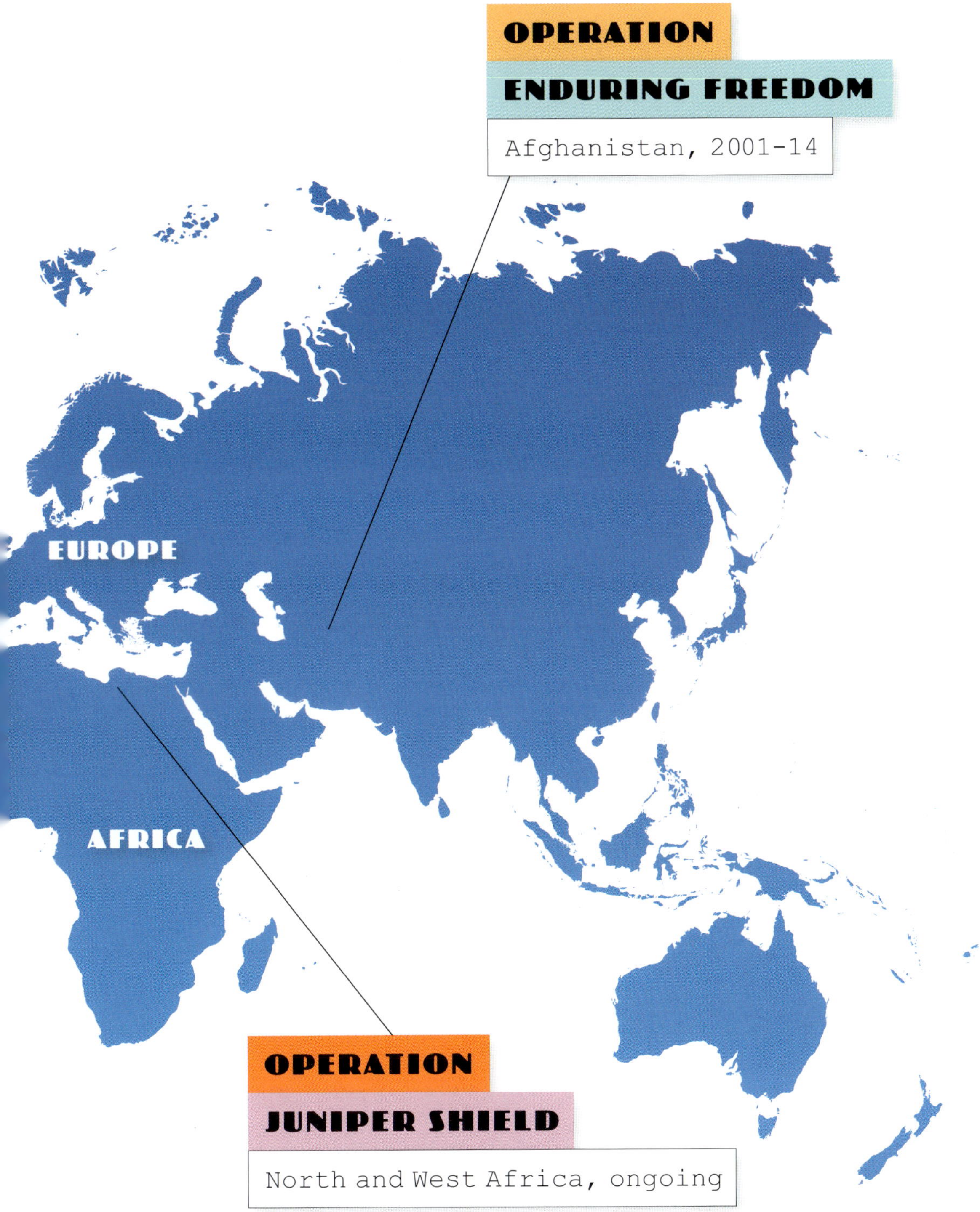
OPERATION
ENDURING FREEDOM
Afghanistan, 2001-14
EUROPE
AFRICA
OPERATION
JUNIPER SHIELD
North and West Africa, ongoing

Tier 1 forces are meant to remain "black," or secret. These include units such as Delta Force and SEAL Team 6. Tier 1 operators may try to blend in with **civilians**. They do not wear uniforms.

Troops who wish to join Delta Force must have at least four years of military experience. They must have at least two years remaining in their enlistment. Officers need a minimum of one year of command experience. Before undergoing Delta Force training, candidates must pass a physical fitness test. It includes 49 pushups, 59 sit-ups, 6 pull-ups, and a 2-mile (3.2 km) run.

Officials do not admit Delta Force exists.

DELTA FORCE BASICS FACT

Past Delta Force code names include Combat Applications Group (CAG) and "The Unit."

TOP FIVE XTREME DELTA FORCE ACHIEVEMENTS

Xtreme Delta Force Achievement #5

Delta Force Fiction The secretive nature of Delta Force attracts many film and television writers. Many movies and shows are based on Delta Force operations. The film *Black Hawk Down* (2001) was based on a book by the same name. It relates the events of the 1993 Battle of Mogadishu in Somalia. In the video game *Call of Duty: Modern Warfare 3*, players can assume the role of Delta Force operators in a variety of missions.

Delta Force is formally known as the 1st Special Forces Operational Detachment-Delta, or SFOD-D.

Delta Force Beginnings

In the late 1960s and early '70s, a wave of terrorist activity swept through Europe and the Middle East. It led many nations to establish elite special forces units. These were dedicated to counterterrorism. Germany formed GSG 9. Britain had the Special Air Service (SAS). The U.S. did not have this type of unit until Delta Force was established.

Colonel Charles Beckwith, of the Green Berets, served with the SAS in the 1960s. Beckwith took command of the newly formed Delta Force in 1977. After 18 months of intense training, the unit was ready for action.

Delta Force had a rough start. In April 1980, the unit attempted Operation Eagle Claw. The goal was to rescue American hostages from Iranian terrorists. The military units involved in Operation Eagle Claw did not communicate well. There were also problems with several of the aircraft needed for the mission. As dust and sand swirled in the air, a helicopter crashed into another aircraft. The explosions that followed killed eight men.

Puerto Rico
1979
Guard duty at Pan American Games

Middle East
1990 to 1991
Gulf War action

Mogadishu, Somalia
1993
Operation Gothic Serpent
Sinaloa, Mexico
2016
Operation Black Swan
BECKWITH

DELTA FORCE BEGINNINGS FACT

Delta Force's first mission was a success. Operators worked as guards during the 1979 Pan American Games in Puerto Rico.

TOP FIVE XTREME DELTA FORCE ACHIEVEMENTS

4

Xtreme Delta Force
Achievement #4

Women of the Unit Delta Force selected female recruits for the first time in 1982. But the selectees were not welcomed by their male peers. The women left the program. Delta Force tried again in the 1990s. Women trained in gathering **intelligence**, defensive driving, and sharpshooting. Male and female operators often work together. This helps the unit blend in with crowds.

XTENSIVE TRAINING

Delta Force's Selection and Assessment course is rigid and demanding. Its training is exhausting. Only a small percentage of candidates make it through the first stages of training.

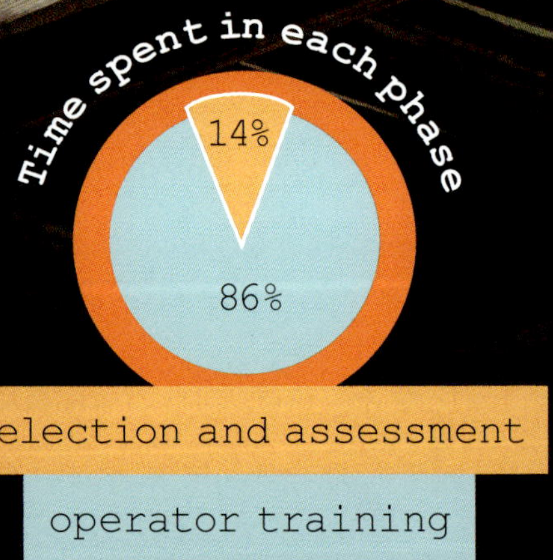

LIFE AS A TRAINEE FACT

Upon successful completion of the physical assessments, further testing determines candidates' mental fitness.

Selection and Assessment

The month-long program weeds out all but the toughest.

Life as a Trainee

The first step to becoming a Delta Force operator is a four-week evaluation. This involves many physical tests. Recruits need to show they are capable of parachuting, scuba diving, and running long distances in all conditions. They do many pushups and sit-ups. Obstacle courses and fully clothed swims present additional challenges.

The final stages are the hardest. Candidates complete a series of land **navigation** tests. The first hike is 6.2 miles (10 km). Trainees wear heavy **rucksacks**. Every day, the marches get longer and the rucksacks are made heavier. These tests are timed. Racing against an unknown clock is one way trainees learn how to handle stress. The final hike is 40 miles (64.4 km). It must be completed alone within 20 hours. These final stages flush out those who are not tough enough.

XPLOSIVE SKILLS FACT

Extensive training helps Delta Force prepare for close-quarters combat.

XPLOSIVE SKILLS

Instructors carefully evaluate candidates. Those who are selected for Delta Force move on to the Operator Training Course (OTC). This six-month training occurs at Fort Bragg.

Operators know many ways of breaching, or breaking into buildings. They may pick locks. Sometimes explosives are necessary.

During OTC, trainees develop skills specific to Delta Force missions. They spend a lot of time learning to make split-second decisions. In "shoot houses," walls can be moved to stage different floor plans. Pictures of either hostages or enemies quickly pop up throughout the house. Trainees must instantly identify targets. They practice similar exercises in aircraft and other tight spaces.

Delta Force operators must be expert marksmen. As trainees, they are required to shoot targets at 600 yards (549 m) with 100 percent accuracy.

TOP FIVE XTREME DELTA FORCE ACHIEVEMENTS

3

Xtreme Delta Force Achievement #3

Battle of Mogadishu In October 1993, the U.S. was involved in Operation Gothic Serpent. Members of various elite special forces units, including Delta Force, planned to capture two enemy leaders. But operators met resistance. Two Black Hawk helicopters were shot down. Fighting continued. By the next morning, 18 U.S. troops had been killed. Dozens more were wounded.

ARCO

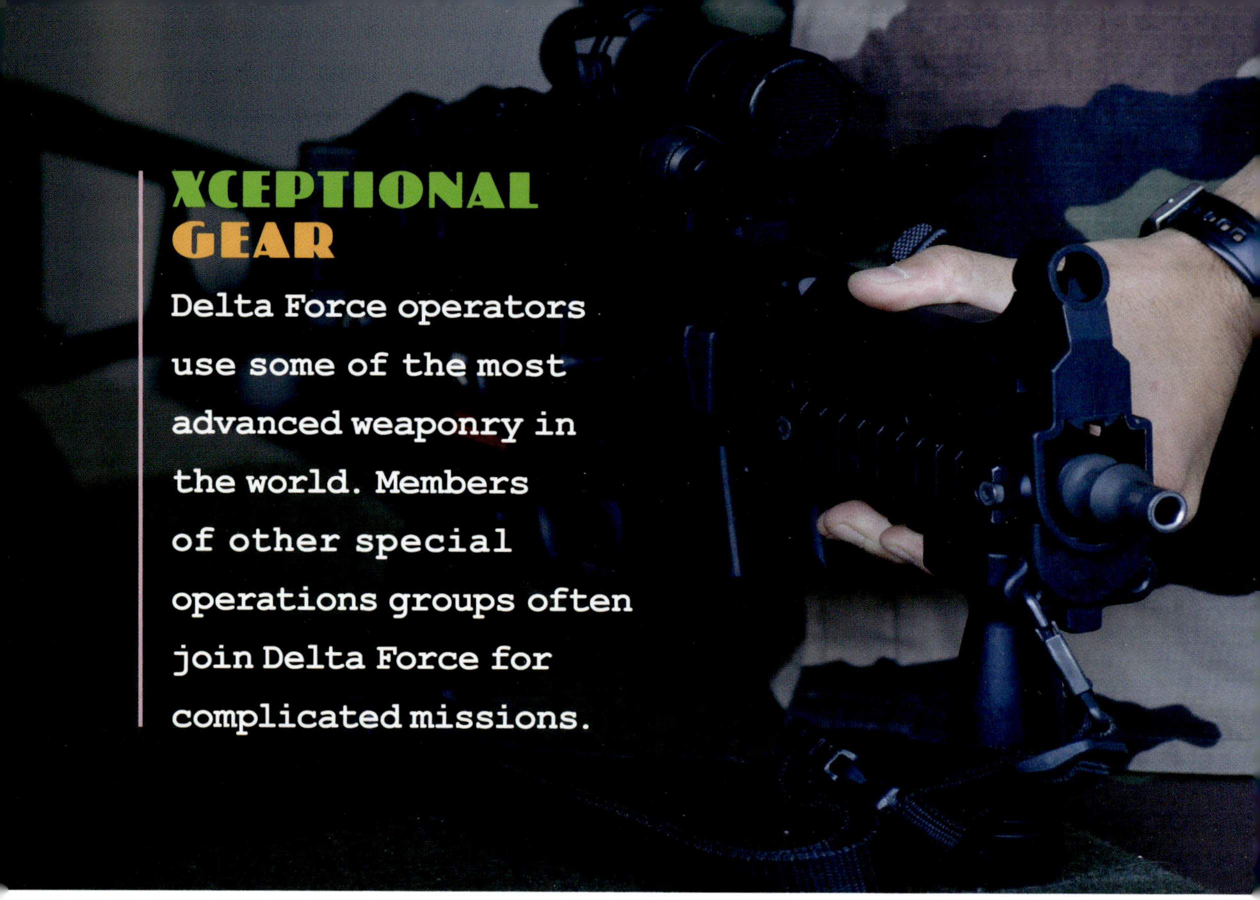

XCEPTIONAL GEAR

Delta Force operators use some of the most advanced weaponry in the world. Members of other special operations groups often join Delta Force for complicated missions.

Delta Force Gear

Unlike most other military units, Delta Force operators are allowed to grow long hair and beards. They usually wear civilian clothes. Sometimes they wear fatigues. But they do not have a designated uniform. Their name, rank, and unit are never displayed.

A Delta Force operator's primary weapon is the HK416 assault rifle. It was designed specifically for Delta Force. This weapon can fire 10 to 15 rounds per second. Operators can add tools, such as a scope or a flashlight, to their guns.

Delta Force operators often rely on the Night Stalkers for assistance. Operators in this special forces unit are helicopter experts. Night Stalkers take other special forces units to target locations. They often drop off and pick up troops at night.

XCEPTIONAL GEAR FACT

Delta Force has an aviation platoon. Its helicopters and airplanes are painted to look like civilian aircraft.

TOP FIVE XTREME DELTA FORCE ACHIEVEMENTS

2

Xtreme Delta Force Achievement #2

Hostage Rescue In April 2004, four Italians were kidnapped by Iraqi criminals. One was killed shortly after. It took months to plan a rescue attempt. On June 8, Night Stalkers flew Delta Force operators over Baghdad. Their target was a house in the suburb of Ramadi. The operators swiftly executed their plan. The kidnappers were caught by surprise. The three remaining hostages and a recently kidnapped Pole were rescued.

XCITING FACTS

Officers wishing to join Delta Force must hold the rank of captain or higher.

Support platoons include signal, aviation, and intelligence-gathering squadrons.

Delta Force actively recruits from all branches of the military in the spring and fall.

Skills developed in the shoot house are utilized during close-quarters combat.

Delta Force operators rarely spare kidnappers' lives during hostage rescue missions.

Delta Force's training facility is sometimes called the "House of Horrors."

Delta Force is believed to have three or four combat platoons.

Operators train with other elite counterterrorism teams, including GSG 9 and SAS.

Trainees practice hostage rescues on buses, trains, and airplanes.

As little as 7 percent of candidates are believed to pass Selection and Assessment.

The final 40-mile (64.4 km) hike is meant to test candidates' mental and physical endurance.

Missions may require only one operator or upwards of a dozen.

Delta Force operators learn to shoot accurately while standing, lying down, walking, and running.

The unit works with foreign governments, as well as other

U.S. special forces, the CIA, and the FBI.

DEA